# THREE BILLY GOATS GRUFF
## A PLAY

Rewritten by ELIZABETH LANE

Illustrated by JIM MADSEN

## CAST OF CHARACTERS
Narrator

Big Billy Goat Gruff

Middle-sized Billy Goat Gruff

Little Billy Goat Gruff

Troll

2

**NARRATOR:**

Once there were three billy goats named Gruff.

All day long they ate grass in a nice, green meadow.

**BIG BILLY GOAT GRUFF:**

*Chomp, chomp.*

**MIDDLE-SIZED BILLY GOAT GRUFF:**

*Munch, munch.*

**LITTLE BILLY GOAT GRUFF:**

*Nibble, nibble, nibble.*

**NARRATOR:**

They ate until the grass was almost gone.

**BIG BILLY GOAT GRUFF:**

We are getting thin.

We need more grass

to chomp and munch and nibble.

**MIDDLE-SIZED BILLY GOAT GRUFF:**

Look at that hillside over there.

It's covered with nice, green grass.

All we need to do is cross that little bridge.

Then we can eat until we are full.

**LITTLE BILLY GOAT GRUFF:**

What are we waiting for?

Let's go!

**NARRATOR:**

Under the bridge lived a mean old troll.

He was taking a nap

when he heard Little Billy Goat Gruff

going *trip-trap*, *trip-trap* across the bridge.

**TROLL:**

Who's that *trip-trapping* over my bridge?

**LITTLE BILLY GOAT GRUFF:**

It is I, Little Billy Goat Gruff.

I'm going to the hillside to eat grass.

**TROLL:**

That's what you think!

I'm going to eat you up!

**LITTLE BILLY GOAT GRUFF:**

Oh! Don't eat me, Mr. Troll!

I'm not big enough for you.

Wait until my brother comes along.

He's much bigger than I am.

**TROLL:**

Bigger? Mmm . . .

Oh, very well, I won't eat you this time.

**NARRATOR:**

So Little Billy Goat Gruff went *trip-trapping* across the bridge to the hillside.

The troll was combing his beard when he heard Middle-sized Billy Goat Gruff going *Trip-Trap, Trip-Trap* across the bridge.

**TROLL:**

Who's that *trip-trapping* over my bridge?

**MIDDLE-SIZED BILLY GOAT GRUFF:**

It is I, Middle-sized Billy Goat Gruff.
I'm going to the hillside to eat grass.

**TROLL:**

That's what you think!
I'm going to eat you up!

## MIDDLE-SIZED BILLY GOAT GRUFF:

Oh! Don't eat me, Mr. Troll!

I'm not big enough for you.

Wait till my brother comes along.

He is biggest of all.

## TROLL:

Biggest? Mmm . . .

Oh, very well, I won't eat you this time.

## NARRATOR:

So Middle-sized Billy Goat Gruff

went *Trip-Trapping*

across the bridge to the hillside.

**NARRATOR:**

The troll was teasing a grasshopper

when he heard Big Billy Goat Gruff going

*TRIP-TRAP*, *TRIP-TRAP* across the bridge.

**TROLL:**

Who's that *trip-trapping* over my bridge?

**BIG BILLY GOAT GRUFF:**

It is I, Big Billy Goat Gruff.

I'm going to the hillside to eat grass.

**TROLL:**

That's what you think!

I'm going to eat you up!

**BIG BILLY GOAT GRUFF:**

That's what YOU think!

**NARRATOR:**

Big Billy Goat Gruff lowered his huge, heavy horns.

Then he started to run.

*TRIPPETY-TRAPPETY*, *TRIPPETY-TRAPPETY*,

*WHAM!* His horns hit the troll.

The mean old troll flew into the air.

He flew over the trees, over the hills,

over the mountains.

When he came down, he was far, far away.

**NARRATOR:**

The three Billy Goats Gruff were happy on the hillside. They chomped, munched, and nibbled until they were full.